"This book is dedicated to my fifth grade teacher for yelling at me about my untied sneakers, and for making me prove that I knew how to tie my own shoes in front of the entire class. I think about that moment routinely. I don't know where you are, but you're still the worst."

Doug is a dung beetle.

Doug was born into a life of shit.
As in he hatched into an actual pile of feces.

Doug doesn't mind because Doug is a big fan of coprophagia. That means he likes to eat poop.

Doug enjoys a variety of excrements,
but he prefers the deuce of an herbivore.

Doug's favorite herbivore is the elephant.
The larger the size, the larger the prize!

Doug often chooses to ride the elephant and wait for the beast to drop a giant dookie so he can get first dibs on that fantastic fecal feast.

Doug likes to play with his food.
He can make a mean shitball.

Since Doug chooses to roll the dung into balls, Doug is considered a roller dung beetle.

Doug can roll over 1,000 times his own body weight. Holy shitballs, Doug is strong!

Doug shows off his muscles and large size
to win the heart of, or at least permission
to mate with, a lady dung beetle.
We'll call her Darla.

Once Doug has sufficiently balled up a big ol' turd, he climbs atop the mass and uses the milky way to get oriented.

Doug rolls his ball-o-shit long distances
to where Darla, the tunneler dung beetle,
is waiting with a freshly carved tunnel.
You can do it, Doug! Roll that shit!

Doug and Darla know their relationship is a bit shitty, but since they have similar hobbies, such as mating and eating fecal matter, it works.

Darla lays the couple's eggs into a
big ball of bowel brownies.

While Darla stands guard over their little dunglets, Doug leaves Darla to journey off and begin the cycle all over again.

Doug is a bit of an absent partner
and a shitty dad.

This process continues for many months...
Eat poop, roll poop, mate in poop, repeat...

Doug is old now.

Wait for it... Wait for it...

Well, shit! Now Doug is dead,
so I suppose that's it.